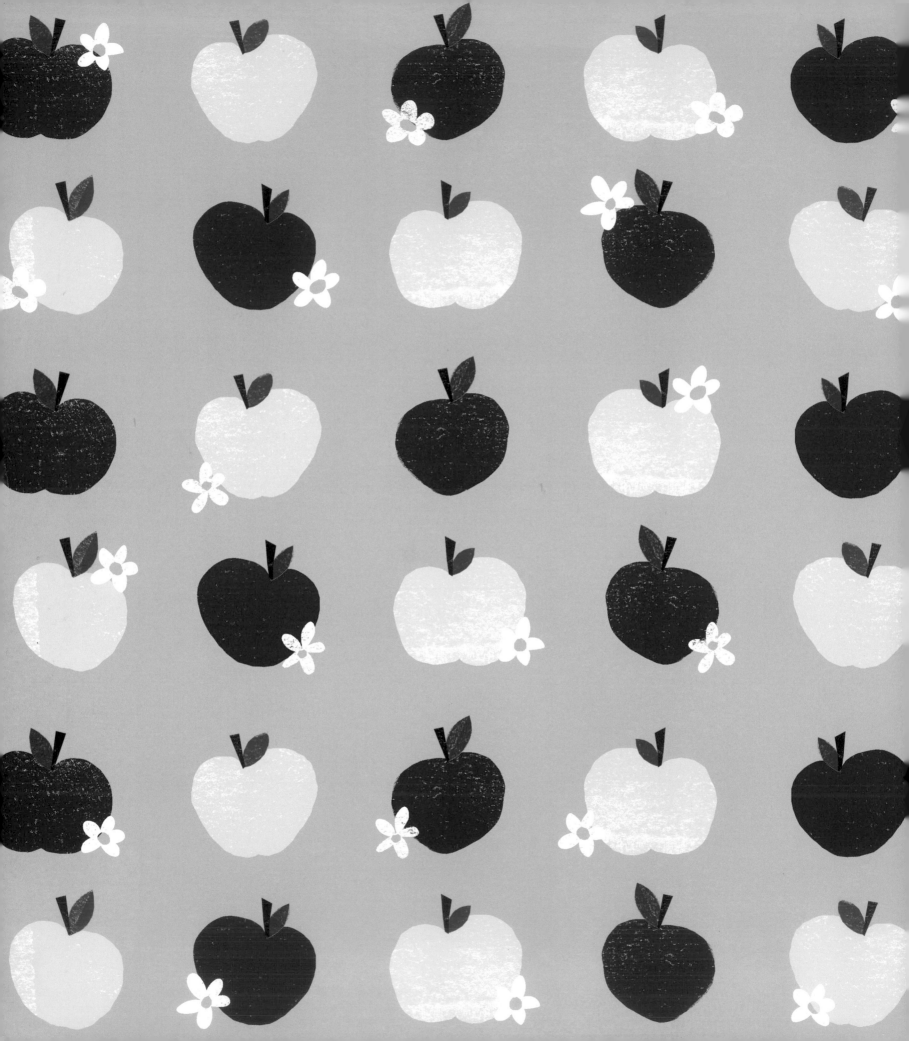

To all the cool cats at
Stillness Infant School – GPJ

For Jill, Jerry and Emma.
Miss you, kiss you – LS

First published in Great Britain 2022 by Farshore
An imprint of HarperCollins*Publishers*
1 London Bridge Street, London SE1 9GF
www.farshore.co.uk

HarperCollins*Publishers*
1st Floor, Watermarque Building, Ringsend Road
Dublin 4, Ireland

Text copyright © Gareth P. Jones 2022
Illustrations copyright © Loretta Schauer 2022
Gareth P. Jones and Loretta Schauer have asserted their moral rights.

ISBN 978 0 7555 0340 7
Printed in the UK by Pureprint a CarbonNeutral® company.
001

A CIP catalogue record for this title is available from the British Library.

MIX
Paper from
responsible sources
FSC™ C007454
FSC
www.fsc.org

This book is produced from independently certified FSC™ paper
to ensure responsible forest management.

For more information visit: www.harpercollins.co.uk/green

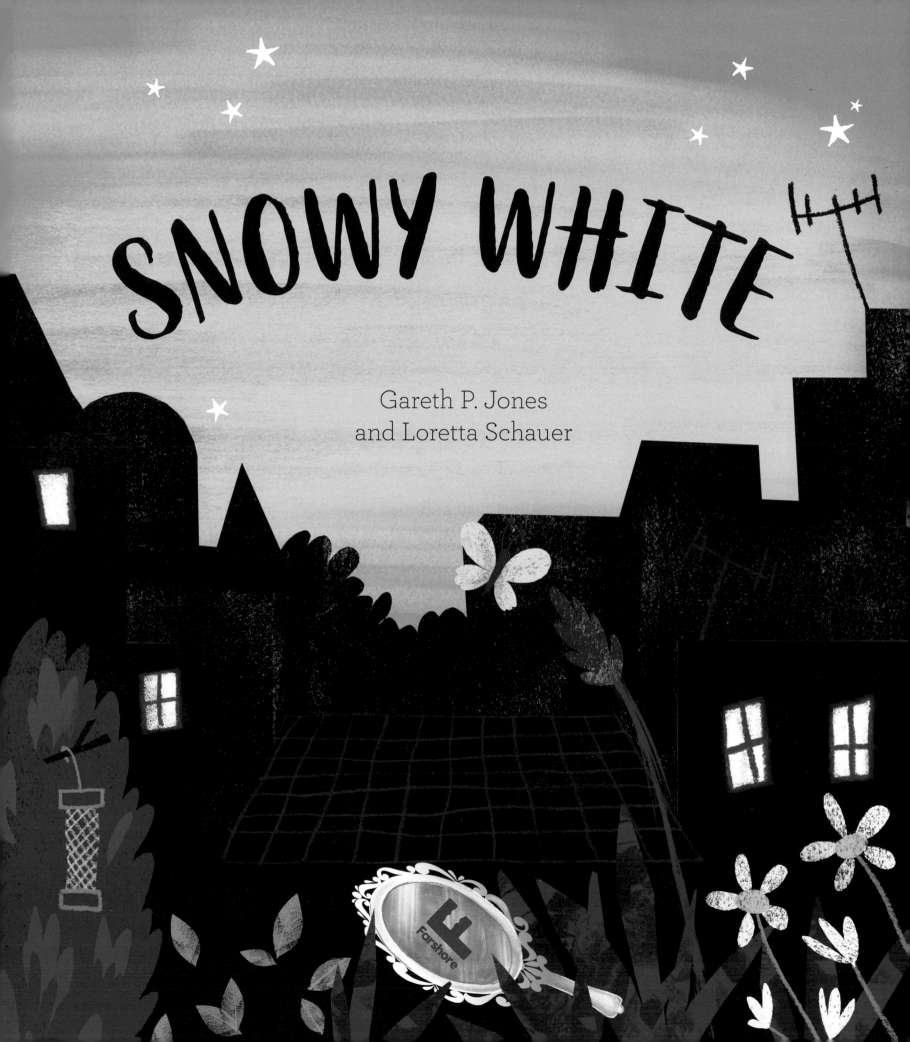

# SNOWY WHITE

Gareth P. Jones
and Loretta Schauer

Once up on a rooftop, above Purry Tale Lane,
there lived a kingdom of cats. They spent
their days preening and cleaning themselves.

Then at night, they took turns
on the catwalk showing off how
splendid they were.

The most purringly perfect puss of them all was a cat called Kingsley.

Kingsley had a crystal ball . . .

or, at least, that's what it said it was.

Every night, Kingsley would ask it:

"Crystal Ball up on the wall,
who's the finest cat of all?"

And it would always reply:

"Kingsley is the best of all,
as sure as I am a crystal ball . . .

And honestly, I *am*
a crystal ball."

One night, a new cat called
Snowy White skated into town.

When Kingsley asked his usual
question, the Crystal Ball replied:

"I saw another cat tonight,
her name, they say, is Snowy White,
Her fur is bright. Her eyes are keen.
The finest cat I've ever seen."

Kingsley cried out:

"It cannot be. I can't have that!
I'll shoo away this rival cat!"

Snowy White was strolling through Purry Tale Lane when she noticed something written on a wall by the old apple tree.

SNOW WHITE
SNOW THANKS.!

SAY NO TO SNOW!

JUST WHISKER AWAY!

TURN TAIL

Snowy spotted Kingsley perched on a high branch.

"Did you write this?" she asked.

Kingsley shook the branch and sent apples raining down on her.

## "Go away! Shoo!"

he yelled.

Snowy White turned and fled, feeling startled — and a bit sticky.

Snowy didn't see the mouse picking up litter until she tripped over him, sending his rubbish bag flying.

"Oh dear. What a pain," said the mouse, "I'll have to pick it up again."

"I'm so sorry. Let me help,"
offered Snowy White.

"A helpful cat? Fancy that!"
squeaked the mouse.

A mouse with a clipboard said:

"We're the Mouse Cleaning Service,
I'm Team Leader Penny Pervis.
If you need cleaning, we're the best,
and now I'll introduce the rest . . .

"Longtail keeps the pond clear,
Fuzzy sweeps the ground.

Charing's an inventor,
using stuff that
Grandma's found.

Chrissie keeps the walls clean,
and then there's me and Michael,

we sort out the rubbish —
it's important to recycle."

"But who makes all this mess?"
asked Snowy White.

"That would be Kingsley and the
catwalk cats," said Penny, pointing
up at the roof.

"Well, I'm new here and I'm not interested
in catwalks. I'd rather help you,"
said Snowy White.

While Snowy White helped the mice, Kingsley and the other cats continued parading up and down the catwalk.

"Just look at the state of her whiskers!" said a ginger cat.

"Don't be so catty!" replied a tabby.

"Oh darling, I love what you've done with your tail," purred a fluffy cat.

None of them noticed the mess they made. None of them cared.

At the end of the night, Kingsley asked:

"Crystal Ball up on the wall,
who's the finest cat of all?"

And the Crystal Ball replied:

"I'm sorry, but again tonight
the finest cat was Snowy White."

Kingsley hissed:

"Snowy White?
SNOWY WHITE!
I will have to put this right!"

As he spun around, his tail accidentally knocked the Crystal Ball off the wall . . .

and it landed with a

SPLASH!

in the water.

Snowy White had spent the night cleaning, so when she spotted Kingsley on a roof she yelled:

"Hey! You up there. Come down here and look at the mess you made last night."

Kingsley made his way down. But when he reached the ground, he couldn't believe his eyes.

"Snowy White?" he said with surprise. "But you're SO grubby! The Crystal Ball called you the finest cat of all."

"Oh, is that what this is? A crystal ball," said Longtail, fishing it out of the pond.

Kingsley turned to the Crystal Ball and said:
"Surely you're not going to tell me that this
scruffy cat looks finer than me?"

And the Crystal Ball replied:

"Kingsley, Kingsley, the catwalk star,
what really matters is who you are.
It's not about looks. It's what you do.
Snowy's beauty shines right through!"

Kingsley listened and he looked. He could see the cats making a mess up high.

He watched the mice cleaning down below. Finally, he understood.

Kingsley bowed his head and said, **"I'm sorry.
I was selfish and mean. But I want to be better."**

"We forgive you,"
smiled Snowy White.

"It sounds like we have a new
recruit!" said the mice.

Kingsley spent the rest of the day helping to tidy up Purry Tale Lane.
When the other cats saw him, one by one, they decided to help.

The more they mucked in,
the muckier they got.

Finally, Purry Tale Lane was clean. So Snowy White and Kingsley threw a party for everyone to celebrate their hard work.

And the Crystal Ball said:

"I'll leave you with this good advice —
be more like these helpful mice.
Clean up your mess, leave none at all . . .

By the way, I'm **NOT** a crystal ball!"

And they all lived happily, purringly —
and considerately — ever after.

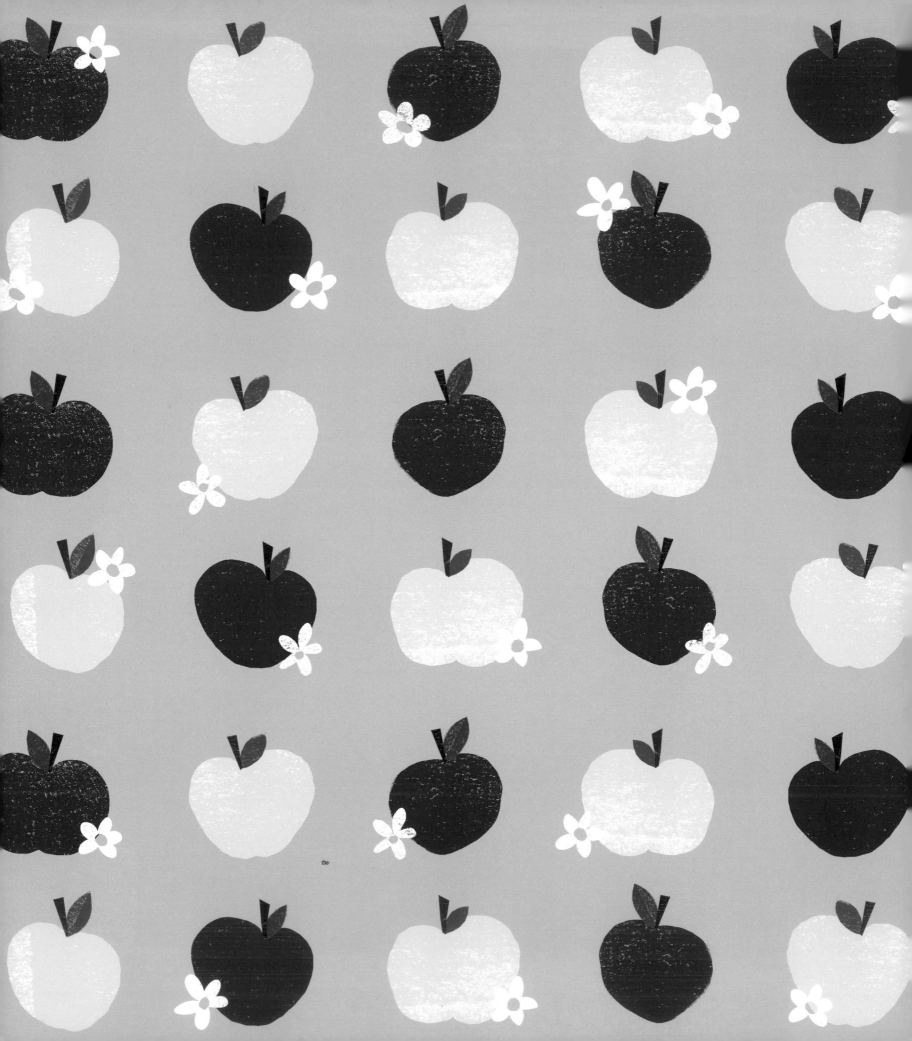

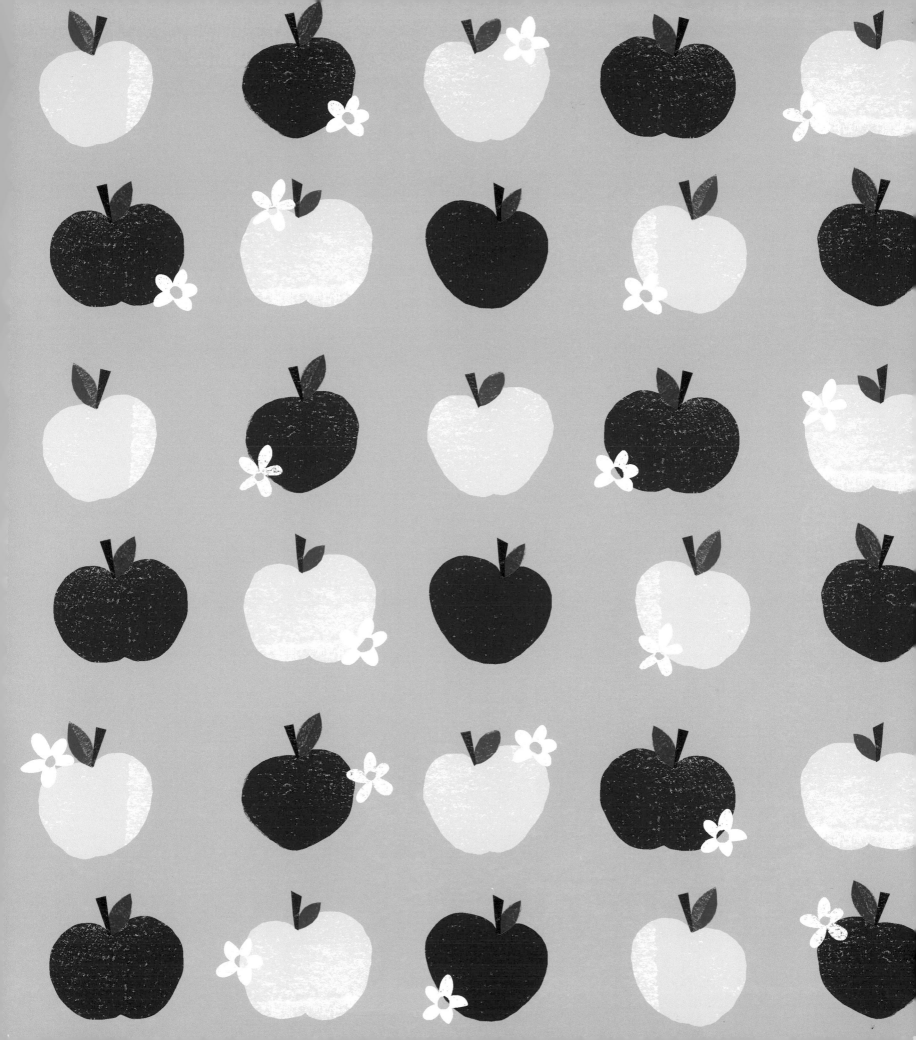